Joan Vegas

BAREBACK ADVENTURES
Hot Threesome Erotica

WARNING

This book contains sexually explicit scenes and adult language. It may be considered offensive to some readers. This book is for sale to adults ONLY.

* * * * * * * * * * * * * * * * * * *

Please store your files wisely where they cannot be accessed by underage readers.

Please feel free to send me an email. Just know that these emails are filtered by my publisher. Good news is always welcome.

Joan Vegas - **joan_vegas@awesomeauthors.org**

You might also want to check my blog for Updates and interesting info.
http://joan-vegas.awesomeauthors.org/

About the Publisher

4Fun Publishing, a member of **BLVNP Incorporated**, 340 S. Lemon #6200, Walnut CA 91789, info@blvnp.com / legal@blvnp.com
NOTE: Due to the highly emotional reaction of some people to works of erotic fiction, any email sent to the above address that contains foul language or religious references is automatically deleted by our anti-spam software and will not be seen. All other communications are welcome.

DISCLAIMER

Please don't be stupid and kill yourself. This book is a work of FICTION. Do not try any new sexual practice that you find in this book. It is fiction and not to be confused with reality. Neither the author nor the publisher or its associates assume any responsibility for any loss, injury, death or legal consequences resulting from acting on the contents in this book. Every character in this book is over 18 years of age. The author's opinions are not to be construed as the opinions of the publisher. The material in this book is for entertainment purposes ONLY. Enjoy.

Bareback Adventures
Hot Threesome Erotica

By: Joan Vegas

© Joan Vegas 2013
ISBN: 978-1-62761-676-8

Author Joan Vegas believes all women (including wives) should have more than one lover, so their lives may be as full and satisfying as possible. Joan lives her beliefs by having a long-term committed relationship with two guys. It is because of her beliefs and her lifestyle that Joan gets lots of letters from other women, men and couples. Those letters are the basis for Joan's books.

This author does not advocate unprotected sex... particularly with strangers. However I have learned that the phenomenon of women (even wives) wanting to experience bareback sex with men other than one's mate is more common than one would think. Without offering judgment, here are the reports from husbands and wives within 18 couples... where the wives have experienced bare cock sex with lovers.

The reports are those actually received by author Joan Vegas in the course of her years-long correspondence with married men and women who enjoy multiple-partner sex play.

Wife's First Lover Took Her Bareback

This story goes back to the first time my wife had some fun with a guy other than me, a guy who we both now call 'her lover.'

By our mutual agreement, the guy was to visit us at our home to make love to my wife. We did meet him a few days before, to make sure my wife and the guy got on OK, and yes, they liked each other.

About 40 minutes before the guy came to our home, I went in to our bedroom and placed four condoms at the side of the bed, so when he was ready to fuck my wife, the condoms would be there for him.

When he walked into our home my wife went over to him, and they started kissing right away. So I went to make some drinks. As I walked back into the living room I discovered that my wife and the guy were locked in an embrace, kissing away like mad. By the sounds my wife was making, she was enjoying it. I was happy to see her enjoying her first new guy since our marriage.

After watching my wife and the guy at the living room doorway for about 5 or 10 minutes, I noticed the guy was feeling my wife's pussy, and she was very turned-on. She then got hold of the guy's hand, and led him up to our bedroom.

I waited in the living room for about 5 more minutes, and then went up to the bedroom. As I went up the steps, I heard my wife making sounds that let me know she was enjoying herself. I was quite pleased.

Reaching the bedroom doorway, I could see my wife lying on the bed. The guy was licking and playing with her pussy. My wife's legs were wide open. Seeing the two of them that way was a massive turn-on for me.

I sat down on the floor at the bedroom doorway to watch the two of them having fun. She was sucking the guy, and I was happy to see he had a good-sized cock. It was thick too. She caught my eye and winked at me.

Then the guy moved in between my wife's legs. I was thinking, 'any second he will get a condom.' But NO, his hand went down to hold his cock. And YES, he then promptly entered my wife's pussy. My heart was beating very fast as I watched his thick cock plunge deep into my wife. By the sounds she was making, my dear wife was loving it!

He was fucking my wife bareback. That was a most erotic thing for me to watch. He has now become her regular lover, and she still always enjoys him bareback.

My wife and I have been talking about bareback fucking quite a bit lately. Although I have seen other guys fuck her, they have always used condoms.

She has never really liked condoms... and never used them with me, or with her previous boyfriends (before we were married). But nowadays she is much more careful, and although she has played around with quite a few guys... she always takes precautions.

But there is one particular guy we have known for years that she has had an ongoing connection with. We all meet up a few times a year for an afternoon of sensual fun. Usually the two of us guys give her long massages, which leads to just her and him exploring further.

They have been getting into Tantra massage, etc. lately, which includes penetration, etc., but she mentioned to me after the last time that she didn't like stopping during the tantric energy buildup just to have him put the condom on. So after much discussion between she and I (and him), we have decided to see how things go next time. Whether he will cum inside her or not is still open... but they are both much happier doing the rest of their Tantric sexual massage without a condom.

For example, when he is giving her a yoni massage with his cock, she says it will feel a lot more sensual and natural. And there are quite a few positions where they lay motionless together, concentrating on breathing and energy, with his cock inside her. She wants to feel the warmth of skin-on-skin, without the condom in between.

One of her favorite positions is sitting on him (either him kneeling up, or him lying down) with her just making very slow movements. I like seeing that too, especially as she guides his cock into her juicy pussy. I decided that would look heaps hotter seeing his cock go into her without a condom on!

So, we will see what happens! She isn't interested in doing bareback with a stranger, etc....but that is fine with me too. A few select guys are satisfying enough for both us.

Bareback Fun with Her Favorite Lover

One of my wife's favorite "extra guys" came over to visit us last evening. She had put on her favorite lingerie, and when he arrived, I made us some drinks. It wasn't long before she took him by the hand and led him to our bedroom, with me following.

When I invite other guys to enjoy my wife's charms, we always insist that they wear condoms. It just seems prudent. However, last night was different. We had decided that this particular lover would be allowed to enjoy her bareback.

First she got his cock hard... sucking it slowly, and ever so carefully licking and tasting every inch of its engorged hard flesh. Once she had him ready, she told him of our decision, and she told him she must have his cock inside her "now!"

She lay back and spread her legs, exposing her wet and willing pussy. He slid the whole length of his stiff cock down and over her clit, rubbing the head a few times over her pussy lips to spread some juices over it so it would go in more smoothly.

She gasped, and told him to stick it inside her pussy. She said she wanted to feel him fuck her. He indulged her and buried his thick cock into her... all in one stroke, and she gasped again. As I watched, he rhythmically fucked her slowly at first. Then he built up speed, all the while she was begging him to fuck her harder.

That was the first time that he fucked her unprotected. She grabbed my cock and started sucking it while moaning from the hard fucking he was giving her. He changed his stroke. I realized she had just squirted all over him, and had one of many orgasms of that night.

He pounded away at her, and I knew from his facial expression it wouldn't be long before he was there too. She stroked my cock with her hand as I watched her pussy get the kind of workout that she loves to feel and I love to watch her get.

He started grunting. He asked once more if it really was OK for him to come inside her. My dear wife replied, "Yes, please squirt it deep inside me. I want to feel your cum deep in my pussy!" He grunted and thrust deeper, as she announced to both of us that she was squirting again.

His strokes slowed down, and became longer, as I saw evidence that both of their juices had mixed... her squirting and his sperm. It was leaking out of her pussy in pulses as he continued to shoot his load up into her unprotected pussy, filling her with his hot cum.

He pulled back, and I watched the tip of his cock (coated with her juices and his cum) slide out. He slid it down the length of her pussy lips, painting her with his cum, as the rest oozed out of her well-used pussy.

I was hard as a rock. I couldn't wait. I shoved my cock into her warm, oozing cum-drenched pussy... where I know it wouldn't be long before I drenched her with my jizz... to mix with his... coating her insides even more with her favorite filling.

Her Lover Had Had a Vasectomy, So She Did Him Bareback

Oh yes, I've seen my wife gobble a bareback cock (often), but until our last threesome we'd not allowed anyone to actually fuck her bareback. That happened about a month ago.

The guy in question had a vasectomy many years ago, and knowing it was one of my wife's fantasies to take another guy's uncovered shaft, we agreed in advance that if the session was going well, we'd let him fill her.

Well, the meeting went quite well. He was open to giving pleasure to, and receiving it from, both of us. When it came time to actually fuck her, I said "no" when he asked if he should put a condom on.

One of his fantasies was to experience the feel of sloppy seconds. I was happy to oblige. She and I pumped each other until I filled her. Then he pressed himself into her just-vacated hole, and soon pumped her to overflowing. It was really erotic to see his cum flowing out of her as we stood and wiped ourselves in front of her spread legs.

I must admit that I had planned to clean both of them up with my mouth, but it had gone on for so long that we had to rush home. So hopefully that'll be next time.

Experienced Extra Guy Loves Going Bareback

I love to fuck a wife bareback while we are being watched by her husband.

I absolutely love to feel her grab my bare, hard cock and guide it into her hot pussy. Then while slowly fucking her, to feel my bare shaft gliding in and out of her wet pussy.

When the pace quickens rapidly, I pull all but my cock head out of her pussy before slamming the whole length of my bare shaft deep inside her. Soon she is grabbing my ass, pulling every inch of my bare fuck tool into her.

When we cannot hold back any longer, I love to drive deep in her wanton hole, as my bare cock spews rope after rope of hot raw cum into her while she orgasms, with her arms wrapped me, pulling me tight against her bare breasts.

That is absolutely the best!

Her Perspective on Bareback Screwing

I have experienced about 10 new cocks, with hubby's permission, in the six years we have been swinging. For me part of the joy of experiencing a new cock is the hot surge of new semen into my cunt or my mouth.

Without that, leading to sloppy seconds, thirds, fourths etc. - the pleasure would be just a fraction of what it is.

A Hubby's Perspective on Watching Wife Fuck Bareback

For the last three-plus years my wife's boyfriend has been fucking her bareback. He has never once put on a condom, and she has never asked him to. Watching him stick his big cock into her, and then blowing his load in her, is always exciting for both of us.

When he leaves, I always get to enjoy the special sensations of sliding my dick into my wife, through his slick seed. What a rush!

Another Perspective on Bareback Fucking of a Wife

We had a threesome recently with a trusted acquaintance. Just as he was about to put the condom on, my wife told him, "No need."

I asked my wife if she really wanted a bareback cock in her, and she said, "Yes." I got to watch him stick his bare cock into my wife's pussy. What a kick to watch his bare cock, coated in my wife's juices, pounding in and out of her. And, both of us got to dump a load in her pussy. Just thinking about that night gets me hard again.

An Unintended Bareback Fuck for His Wife Leads to More

Here's a true bareback report. My wife and I went to a local bar where we ended up meeting a nice young man. He and my wife hit it off, and after a few drinks they were having a good time grinding on the dance floor.

After the bar closed, he brought up the idea of going back to his place. We agreed to join him at his place, and had a few more drinks. During that time my wife explained to him that I was okay with her fooling around, and that we'd had threesomes before. He said he'd been in a few before too, and asked the rules.

We told him pretty much anything goes, as long as he uses a condom during intercourse. We let him know she was not on the pill. Soon, his hands were wrapped around her ass as they embraced. He was feeling under her skirt as he explored her mouth with his tongue. She began to undo his pants and pull out his hard cock. It was a nice size, about 7 inches.

He was a body builder, and had a completely shaven crotch, which I could tell she liked. I sat on the couch watching, and she began to lick his cock all the way down his shaft to his balls. Soon she had a nice rhythm going as her head bobbed up and down.

I figured he was ready to take things further, because he suddenly picked her up and carried her into his bedroom. He grabbed a condom, and spread her legs apart. I love watching the head of another man's cock slide into my wife's pussy for the first time. She moaned as it disappeared inside her.

They fucked in several positions for the next hour or so. Things kind of slowed down, and I asked if they wanted another drink? They said yes, and off I went to the kitchen. I wasn't gone long, but I guess long enough for things to get started again.

I came back to find my wife laying naked on top of him... only that time I could see he didn't have a condom on. I figured he must have pulled her onto the bed after I left. He was holding her tight against him, grinding his bare cock against her shaven pussy. I instantly got hard as I walked in on them.

They were so caught up in the moment that they were totally un-aware that I was back. I quietly watched as my wife reached down, grabbed his bare cock and guided it into her wet pussy. It slid right in, and she let out a little moan.

For a second, I thought about stopping them, but the scene was too damn hot to stop. I was finally getting to see my wife take another man's cock bareback.

He began fucking her harder, pulling her ass tight. My wife was moaning her way to a deep orgasm. She bounced her pussy up and down on him. She threw her head back and hissed her internal pleasure. Her orgasm just seemed to take over her body.

As she was relishing the pleasures coursing through her body, he continued to pump... until I saw his back arch up, pressing himself deeply into my wife's love cavern.

Suddenly, she must have realized what was happening. I am sure she felt the powerful squirts of his hot sperm inside her. That brought her back to reality. She quickly pulled off of him, went to his bathroom, and tried to wash herself out.

On the way home she had me stop at a drug store so she could get a "Day After" pill. Fortunately, she did not get pregnant from that encounter.

Since neither of us wants kids yet, she decided to see a doctor and get a birth control implant in her vagina. After that night she told me that it was really "hot" to have that guy erupt inside her... and that she would really like to do that again, now that she doesn't have to worry about pregnancy.

Since then my beautiful wife has enjoyed nearly a dozen more guys... all bareback... with me enjoying her new pleasures with her.

My Husband Arranged a Special Bareback Night for Me

My husband shared me bareback with one of his friends one night. I had always said that I would do it once... and that would be it. However I did enjoy it. So we started talking about who was going to cum inside me next.

I love when my husband cums inside me, feeling his cock pulse and jerk... and watching his face turn red as he empties in me. Oh yes, I do love it. But at first I didn't like the thought of other men cuming inside me. I thought that treat was just for my husband to have. My husband had often shared me with other guys and once even three young studs at the same time... but always with condoms.

After a long time of him asking me to let someone do me bareback, I did it that first time, and I have to admit I liked the way it felt. So after our chats, I decided that I wanted to have all my young studs over for a bareback night, with no one else (except my hubby). He arranged it. To my surprise the three of them phoned me all week, telling me they couldn't wait to have me. They were talking dirty to me on the phone.

I'm going to describe them to you. "F" is my favorite. He is very loving when he touches me, and he has a to-die-for body. "R" is a black guy with a gorgeous body and a great personality. He makes us laugh a lot with his comments. What a mover he is. He always turns up with a present for me, talks to me, treating me like a lady. But Jesus Christ he fucks with intensity! Last but not least is "B". He is lovely, and has an extra thick cock.

The Saturday we had arranged for the guys to come over, we had an unexpected visit by one of our kids. That set us both on edge, and we nearly cancelled our night. But our daughter left. That was good, because my husband had not been able to reach the guys to warn them.

I ran upstairs, jumped in the shower, and got dressed. I wore a purple and black underwear set, stockings, suspender/garter belt, matching panties and bra. I covered it over with a dress that wraps round and ties closed.

F was first to arrive as usual, and stood with a drink in the living room with me, while my husband answered the door. We were kissing when R came into the room. As usual, he presented me with a gift. As I took it, he wrapped his big arms around me and kissed me passionately, pushing his tongue almost down my throat. Then B came in, getting a drink from my husband before coming over to kiss me.

"So, I understand we are all cuming bareback inside you tonight, babe," said R.

Before I had a chance to respond, F had me in his arms and was kissing me. He removed my dress, while feeling my tits and nipples. R moved behind me and licked my rear cheeks, moving them apart. His tongue found my anus, and he licked hard at it, trying to push the tip of his tongue inside. He stopped for a minute and striped off my thong, my garter belt, and stockings, before he moved in again, pulling my ass checks apart. He likes rimming my anus. F was by then finger-fucking my pussy, as my husband joined in.

I removed my bra for him to feel my tits, play with my nipples, and kiss my shoulders. I felt for a cock, but not one was out yet. Still being kissed by F, and not wanting it to stop, I moved my hands to his face. The boys, all in their twenties (I am 39), made me weak at the knees.

One finger turned to two as R took over the fingering of my pussy. F moved to my nipples, with his mouth licking, flicking, and sucking at them. I looked over to my husband who was taking photos. I called him to kiss me. As he did, the boys stopped. I thought they were stripping... but no.

F pushed me down on the table, still dressed, with me naked as the day I was born. He pulled his cock out and slowly pushed it into me without a condom covering it. Oh my god his uncovered cock felt so good! F has a beautiful cock, big but not too big. It was hard, but soft to touch. He slowly fucked me in front of everyone. When I say 'fucked me,' he didn't... he made love to me, while still dressed and feeling my tits. The other two joined us, licking my nipples and kissing me. F just kept going slowly.

"OH YEA, OH FUCK... QUICK... OH MY FUCKIN GOD! HOLY FUCK," I screamed as he kept the same tempo. His bare cock felt so good! I exploded! That was what I call an orgasm. It was heaven. It just kept going on and on. Shivers ran through me and all over me as he kept going. I could feel his cock pulsing inside me. I knew he was going to cum. I thought he was going to speed up, but he didn't.

Then he slowed almost to a stop. "Oh fuck, what a cunt," he said. "I love your pussy, I love you." As he spoke, he was cuming inside me. He had all but stopped his movement within me, to make sure I could feel his cum. I was lying back on the table, legs being held up, and his balls just pumped his cum into me.

"Can you feel me cuming inside you?" he asked.

"Of course I can babe," I told him. As he kissed me, his swollen cock reduced. He was pushed to the side by R. My pussy must have been dripping with F's cum, but R just pushed on in there, and I was back to being fucked... and boy can F fuck. He goes like a train. The sweat starts on his forehead, then drips, landing on me.

My legs were over his shoulders, and he was banging me as if possessed. Fuck, he can go! He sped up. His cock pulsed and seemed to get harder. "This time we cum together, baby," he said, as he finished off with a couple of extra pushes and stood up. My husband was next.

"Your cunt is soaking." He was stating the obvious.

"That's what happens when guys cum inside your wife's pussy bareback," I told him. He lay over me, licking my nipples, as I felt the guys' cum running down my legs. I asked my husband, "Did you watch these young guys cum inside your wife? Can you feel their cum with your dick? I can feel it running down my legs."

I don't know why it turns my husband on so much, but it always makes him cum sooner when I talk like that. Quickly, he was number three to cum inside me. He pulled out and lifted me onto the couch. He stuck his dick up to my mouth. It was covered in cum. I removed most of it with my hand before I took it into my mouth for a good suck. B was next. As I sucked my husband, B knelt down and pushed his cock into my pussy. My tits were being felt up, my husband's stiff cock was in my mouth, my cunt was full with a fourth cock, and I had cum running out and down my legs.

That went on all night. They took turns fucking me, banging me, and all of them emptying their cum inside me multiple times. F was the only one to cum in my mouth. The rest all just came in my pussy. Of course I came numerous times myself... I mean REALLY came! I loved the whole night. By 2 AM, my cunt hole, pussy lips, nipples, and arse were really tender. The guys were all well spent too, so they said their goodnights.

F decided to stay the night, but I told him, "No more." He kissed me gently, and retired to our spare room.

My husband told me, "You were fucked about twenty times tonight, and each time we all came in you."

He felt my very wet pussy. I told him, "She is tender, and she needs some time to herself."

Once I was in my bath, my husband came in naked, and jumped in the shower. When he came out drying himself, he picked up the washcloth and washed my shoulders. Then he ran the cloth down my front, running over my boobs and swollen nipples. I let him wash me because he always does that very gently, running the soap and his hands all over my body.

F has had me nearly every day since that night, with and without my husband, and now he always cums inside me… bareback of course. I love it.

SO, all in all, I think I have gotten quite comfortable with the bareback thing. Actually, I love it!

AnonyMrs.

Skin on Skin Is Best

I love the way my lover feels inside me with no rubber, just skin on skin... his cock head spreading my lips open, me letting him into my body. My husband loves to watch as my lover pounds his bare cock into my cunt over and over, fast and hard, then slow and soft... just repeating it all different ways.

Then, as my loving hubby holds me in his arms, my lover and I approach the moment I have been waiting for... that's me feeling his cock spasm inside me, and then him filling me full of his cum. I just love that wet warm feeling.

Nothing excites me more than when my bareback connection is with someone I've just met. It's just not good sex for me unless he cums deep in my pussy at least once.

I know that moments later, as quickly as my lover withdraws from my body, my dear hubby will drive himself into me, enjoying 'sloppy seconds'. As my lover cuddles with me and kisses me... I know my hubby will treat me to a delicious orgasm before adding his cream to that which is already inside me.

I Love Bareback Sex

My husband loves to share me with his male friends and occasional strangers. I have come to love it too. But I feel more of a connection with our bedroom guests when I have that skin-to-skin contact. Nothing compares.

There is no doubt about it for me anyway, bare is the only way I want my lovers inside me. As my husband knows, sometimes I have not been on the pill when he has treated me to MFM pleasures. Those times have always given my hubby and me an extra rush, more pleasure... knowing our risk of our guest implanting a baby in me.

The conflict of wanting pregnancy, and yet not really wanting it at that time with that sperm donor, makes me so incredibly hot. Sometimes I have practically screamed when I felt the hot cream of a guest lover filling me. I just melt and shake and moan all at once.

On those occasions my insides go crazy from it, with what feels like tight contractions in my vagina, and even in my uterus. My body just seems to want the guest lover's seed deep inside, to make us a baby.

A baby resulting from play with a guest lover would be just awful for us, but that is why it just adds to my thrills when I get a beautiful bare guy to pump me full. My husband and I know I am nuts, and could result in me getting knocked up if I continue, but I just adore it so.

Lover's Lube Is His Turn-On

Bareback sex is a must for my wife. When we are playing, seeing a guy on top of her, pounding her pussy until he can't take any more, then unloading into her is the utmost turn-on. Having her after him is a treat, using another man's cum as lube, feeling her filled pussy... there is just nothing better than seconds, when it's within your own wife.

Unknown Father

My husband and I had been discussing having a second child. Our first was a darling girl, and she was about 2½ when we had our discussion. I had been back on the pill, and of course after our discussion I stopped taking it. A couple months passed, and when I didn't get preggers, we just stopped worrying about it... and thought if it happened, then it would happen.

During that same time I was having a hubby-approved affair with the VP in my company, and we fucked very regularly in his office. I had been fucking him bareback for quite a few months before going off the pill, and I just kept having unprotected sex with both he and my husband, hoping to get pregnant eventually. To be truthful, I pretended that I didn't care if my husband or my boss knocked me up, as long as I got pregnant, but in retrospect I think I really wanted to have my boss's baby.

Anyway, after a few more months I did get pregnant, and when I told my boss, he showed his true colors... he wanted me only for sex, and was afraid that I would claim him as the father.

I had no intention of doing that, and when my second baby girl was born, my husband was thrilled. I was somewhat relieved to see that the person she grew up to resemble most was me. But I really don't know who the bio-father is.

Another Unconventional Pregnancy

My wife and I already had a child. My wife is very desirable, and men seemed to be easily attracted to her. With my approval, she had an affair with a guy she had met at work. I have always liked the fact that she is so desirable to other men.

Soon I became a very willing cuckold, and she let me know she did not want to use condoms or other forms of protection during her sex play with other men. Over the years my wife has now been pregnant five times by four different men. She miscarried the last three.

Our second and fourth children were fathered by other men. Both of the fathers knew they had impregnated her. The later one came to see his child as a baby several times, before drifting out of our lives. The children are all grown up now and married themselves. They are unaware they have different fathers.

Planning for Their Future

My fiancé and I are planning to get married October 2014. For now, we are both in college. While in college, with my encouragement, she is trying her hand at experiencing sex with different men of varying age, race, color, and size. We are not actively trying to get her pregnant yet (she's on the pill), but she is experimenting with barebacking strangers.

We have decided that our wedding date will be set for when she is ovulating. She will be off the pill by then. We plan that after our beautiful ceremony and reception, there will be a private reception… just for male guests.

She has not yet given me a number yet, but it seems she would love to have a group of men available for that private gathering… to take her, and to fill her bareback. That way she can, and will, carry a child from our wedding night... just not necessarily mine.

We are both really turned-on by our plan.

Bareback Lovers Have Fathered Two of Her Children

My husband and I enjoy me having sex with other men (particularly well-endowed men). Sometimes I have them use condoms (especially when the relationship is new or I am menstruating), but I much prefer the feel of a bare cock against the lips of my pussy and the walls of my vagina or ass... or in my mouth for that matter.

As a result, I have often let my boyfriends fuck me bareback... even during my more fertile periods of the month. As a result, two of my three children were fathered by two of my boyfriends. My husband has not been fucking me since I've started having men with bigger cocks fuck me, so, when we decided to have more children, he was more than happy to let other men impregnate me.

Neither my children nor our family know our secret, and we have no intention of telling them. Likewise, I have never told my boyfriends that they are my kids' real fathers.

I Impregnated My Married Lover

I am from Belgium. I work for a Dutch-based company that has offices in a variety of countries around the world. After working for them for two years, they transferred me to Southeast Asia... the exotic Far East.

Shortly after arriving at my new post I met a sexy young English married woman who was working in our office. We began to flirt and share our lunches together. Of course I knew she was married, but nevertheless it was not long before we became lovers.

We would meet up on weekends and go to a special place we had found in the countryside. There we would make love in a beautiful warm plunge pool of a waterfall. She was a charmer... blonde, blue eyes, pretty face, big tits and fantastic, child-bearing hips that had a tight pussy framed by blonde wispy pubes.

Every time we met we fucked like rabbits... always bareback. She couldn't seem to get enough of my cock, and I loved filling her cunt with my fertile sperm. I fucked her so deeply that sometimes I could feel her protective coil on my cock, which hurt us both. But knowing my cock was nudging at the entrance of her cervix was a very erotic feeling for us both.

One time I said to her, "What if I dislodge your coil and plant my seed right inside you, and get you pregnant?" She just laughed. But the though had been put into her mind.

I loved sending her home to hubby with my spunk cascading from her pussy, soaking into the crotch of her panties, and sometimes leaking down her thighs... she had taken that much sperm from me.

She typically had to sneak in the house and go straight in the shower and flush her pussy out, just in case her hubby wanted her body when she got in from a day of allegedly walking in the hills.

She was 23 and I 33, both fertile people. Her hubby was 29. She told me one day that she and her husband had decided to try for kids, and that therefore she couldn't fuck me anymore... and in fact didn't want to see me whilst they were trying. I was horrified, but accepted her decision. She was the best fuck I had ever had, and still is today. I was going to miss our lovemaking badly.

A few months came and went, and nothing had happened. She hadn't been knocked up. As we worked together too, it was frustrating as I saw her every day... that pretty sexy girl. I started to dream about making her preggo myself, visualizing her swelling belly from my insemination, and still being allowed to fuck her as our child grew inside her womb.

I think preggo women are the sexiest thing to walk the planet... swollen breasts, perky dark brown nips, round ass... and of course that sexy extended tummy and belly button. I stare at them all the time if I see one in public. I always try to get a glimpse of a tit, nipple, or a bare belly... such an erotic sight.

One night at a company party we were both attending we eventually got to chat in private. I asked her how they were doing. She blushed and said, "Not well. Hubby is having a hard time keeping it up, and hasn't been fucking me often enough or at the right time." She also said she missed me terribly, and had been having wet dreams about me inseminating her.

I stared straight into her blue eyes and said, "I could get you pregnant by the time your next cycle comes around, and you know it."

"I know," she said.

So I said, "What about it? Meet me at our spot on Sunday, and I will fuck you all day. I too have been dreaming about getting you pregnant with 'our' child. I want to give you a child. Let me do it." I could see she was getting aroused, her nips were poking through her blouse, and her face flushed.

I was hard. I took her hand and placed it on my cock so she could feel it. She looked around the room to see if anyone was watching, and then pushed down on my crotch and rubbed me harder. There was a mischievous glint in her eye, so I took a gamble and pulled her to a private area outside. She came willingly. We didn't care. By then we just wanted to rut like mating animals. It had being so long since we last fucked.

Through the car park were some trees that gave us cover. I pushed her up against a tree and we stared to snog... deep French kissing, tongues fighting each other. My cock ached as she pulled down my trousers and pants, and was thankful for its release into her hand.

It was clear to both of us... we were there to fuck, and nothing else (no foreplay) was required. I knew she would be ready for me, and as I slipped my fingers into panties they found her gushing like our waterfall. I flipped her round and she took hold of the tree trunk.

Lifting her dress, I saw her ass framed by her black thong. I just pulled it to one side, took hold of my bare cock, found her entrance, rubbed it along her labia to lubricate its head, and pushed in. She swallowed my bare cock inside her unprotected cunt, and I slammed all the way into the hilt. What a wonderful feeling!

She reached behind, taking my balls in her hands as if feeling their weight for sperm. She said, "Impregnate me, Ian. Make a baby in me... please. Fill me up with your spunk. I want to feel you ejaculate all the way inside my womb. Fuck me deep... and cum inside me."

Hearing her say that sent me over the edge. I slammed into her and whispered in her ear, "I'm cumming!" She reached back for my arse and tried to pull me deeper into her cunt and hold me as I spurted my baby-making seed into her unprotected womb. I felt her body quake through an orgasm.

"I can feel you spurting inside me," she said, as she counted 8 or 9 spurts from me. "Fucking hell Ian, how much have you got inside those balls, babe?"

I held her against the tree quite firmly to stop her from moving. I kept my cock in her to the hilt, to stop my sperm from leaking out, letting my last drops seep into her pussy and swim for her eggs... to consummate the coupling we were enjoying. Her body shook again.

As my cock relaxed and flopped out, I held my hand in place over her swollen, open pussy, to keep my sperm inside her. I turned her around. She was crying. "What's up, babe?" I said.

"Oh Ian... I just climaxed as I felt your sperm inside me," she replied. "It was a beautiful feeling. I just couldn't help it."

We sneaked back in to the party and went our separate ways that night. We kept stealing glances at each other. I watched her standing next to her hubby, and kept thinking 'there she stands, her womb filled with my sperm, spunk filling the gussett of her thong and leaking down her thighs... and hubby is blissfully unaware that my sperm are making their way into her womb... getting his wife pregnant with our child'.

To cut a very long story short, I did knock her up that night. Nine months later she had a baby boy. I was able to fuck her throughout her pregnancy, and we both loved it. Watching her body grow into motherhood, and sucking on her milk-laden breasts was an awesome thing. The boy is now 18, and her hubby is none the wiser.

This is a true report.

The End

Here is a sample from another story you may enjoy:

JOAN VEGAS

Scottish Affair

A SCOTSMAN SHARES HIS WIFE

HOT THREESOME EROTICA

I have been working hard on getting my wife to allow me to share her with other guys, and my investment is now paying off.

After much encouragement, she finally fucked Ian, an ex-colleague (now close friend)… with my complete consent. The only downside was that I didn't get to see it, but she openly told me all about her first romp with a man other than me since our marriage.

Keen not to pressure her, I haven't gone on about it, but I have told her how much I enjoy this new part of our life. I've also suggested that I would love to see her having fun. I let her know that although I would be happy with just watching, I would also participate, if she wished.

On a recent Saturday, Ian phoned her for a chat. Without warning, I heard her invite him to pop in later that evening for a few drinks. Even though I could only hear her side of the conversation, it was obvious he wasn't sure. I heard her say, "No, it'll be fine," and, "Honestly, I told you he's OK with it."

After the call finished she gave me a naughty smile, a quick kiss, and asked what I wanted for dinner. I didn't want to badger her to find out if she had anything in mind, or if this was just a social visit, but I couldn't help feeling more than a little excited.

Later that evening, Ian arrived at our door. I wasn't sure what to do, as I thought just me greeting him at the door might seem slightly intimidating, but me sitting on the couch as he walked in could also be awkward. In the end, I stood slightly behind and to the side of my wife as she answered the door.

He said hello, and she leaned in to kiss him as he stepped over the threshold. As soon as she drew away I put out my hand to shake his, with a friendly, "Hi Ian. How's u?" He replied, "Um, yeah fine thanks." I asked what he wanted to drink, and wandered off to pour up some drinks for us all.

There was an initial slight awkwardness as we sat and chatted, although my wife was quite relaxed and chatty. After a few drinks though, we were all laughing and joking... and any strangeness was gone. There was no reference to what we all knew had happened earlier between them, and I still had no idea where the evening might lead, although I was secretly hopeful.

As the evening wore on my wife was clearly becoming merrier as the drinks flowed. I had made a point of ensuring we had plenty available. I hoped it would help us all relax, perhaps lose any awkward inhibitions, and knowing full well the effect that alcohol has on my lovely wife. Apart from making her consistently horny, a few drinks will generally get her into a flirty and more openly suggestive mood.

A few hours into the evening, I had gone to the kitchen to pour up another round. My wife joined me. Nuzzling up to me from behind, she whispered into my ear, "Well, the wine is having its usual effect on me." I turned around and she kissed me before saying, "Do you still want to see?"

I hoped I knew what she was talking about, but felt I should make sure. "See what?" I asked, my throat cracking as I said the words.

She smiled and drew closer, "See me have sex with him..." Her voice lowered as she whispered, "Do you want me to fuck him while you watch?"

As she spoke, my heart leapt, and my already swelling cock began to twitch. "Yes," I said, "You know I'd love that." I felt her hand slip down and cup my crotch as she smiled and said, "MMMM, I think you really would." She kissed me and returned to the lounge, sitting on the couch opposite Ian, but slightly closer than before.

I returned, sat down, and she smiled at me as I passed her drink. I wasn't sure what would happen, but was sure it would be a fun evening either way. We carried on talking, and the tension was killing me as it seemed that time had slowed down.

My wife reached into her handbag, pulled out her phone and said, "Ian, you've got a Blackberry, haven't you?" He looked confused for a moment, then confirmed that he did. She said, "Do you know how to change the screensaver? I can't figure out how to do it at all." He responded, "Yeah, no problem, I'll show you how."

With that, she stood, took a few steps and sat beside him, then passed him the phone. He quickly showed her how, and asked what she wanted as her background. She scrolled through, found a picture, and selected it as she passed the phone back to him. He looked down at the phone, gulped, and looked at me before looking slightly awkward for the first time since he'd arrived. She quickly piped up, "Do you like that one Ian?" Nervously he stuttered before replying, "Erm, yes... it's, err great".

She retrieved the phone before turning it around so I could see. Despite the Blackberry's small screen, I could clearly see it was a photo of her lying naked in bed, with her full back and bum exposed, on which I'd used a Photoshop filter to give it the appearance of a painting.

I looked over at my wife and I saw the kind of wicked smile I'm very used to seeing when she's slightly (or very) drunk and feeling quite frisky. I looked down and noticed she had her hand on Ian's thigh, and I suspected he hadn't quite noticed as he was so caught up in the strangeness of viewing my wife's naked picture while I was there. The fact that he knew I knew he'd fucked her a couple of weeks prior probably added to his momentary unease.

My wife giggled and said, "Nothing you haven't already seen Ian," as she gave his thigh a squeeze. Obviously unsure what was happening he said, "Erm, yes... it's a lovely painting... very nice."

My wife smiled and said, "Ian, he knows (as she nodded toward me), and he's fine with it. In fact he suggested it. Although I kinda chose who it would be." Ian looked quickly at her, then at me. I smiled, but tried not to show either how nervous or excited I was before confirming, "Its fine Ian, seriously I'm fine with it all."

Her hand found his cheek as she whispered, "Don't worry," before moving closer and softly kissing him full on his lips. He took a few moments before responding and starting to kiss her back. As the minutes passed and they continued kissing, he appeared to become more comfortable with what was happening.

His hand gripped my wife's waist and pulled her closer to him. His hand moved back and forth along her waist as if he was unsure how to proceed, before she guided his hand to her breast. As he cupped her breast, I heard her breathing change, and she squeezed his hand around her beautifully full breast.

I sat unsure what to do. Part of me felt I should leave them for a few moments, but I was transfixed watching my wife kissing another guy a few feet away from me, and the kisses becoming breathier and more passionate. I decided to sit back and quietly enjoy my drink. I noticed that I had been sitting with my hand resting on my crotch, and only realised when I gave myself an unconscious squeeze, as if to mask the swelling I was experiencing.

Looking back over toward them, I saw my wife starting to undo her top, unbuttoning it without breaking their kissing even for a moment. In a single movement, she reached behind her and undid the clasp at the back before guiding his hand back to her breast, pushing his hand up and under her undone bra. I heard her gasp as his hand touched her tender skin, and the familiar noise she makes when her nipples are touched.

As he brought his head down to her exposed breast, he gently lifted it toward his face before placing her nipple into his mouth and gently sucking on it. She pushed him back onto the couch and he broke away for a moment, possibly wondering if she was stopping him. Lifting her arms, she pulled her top back and off, quickly followed by her bra, which she tossed onto the floor as she started to kiss him again before sitting astride his legs.

The sight of my wife naked from the waist up, writhing as she kissed him was incredible to watch. He quickly lifted both hands to caress her breasts before she guided his head down where he started kissing and nuzzling them, all the time never letting go of her tits.

I was suddenly aware that I was still squeezing the developing bulge at the front of my trousers as she looked round and said, "Is this still what you want? " My mouth was dry as I croaked a barely audible, "Yes."

"And you're happy for us to do more?" she questioned me. I again replied, "Yes..." before adding "...as much as you want."

She smiled and groaned slightly as Ian sucked on her nipples. "Thank fuck," she said. "There's no way I could stop now!"

If you enjoyed this sample then look for <u>Scottish Affair.</u>

Also by this Author

About the Author

Joan Vegas was born in 1973 and grew up in a small town in mid-USA. After graduating from college, she met two guys. Both were really special and she fell in love with both of them.

She was fortunate that they love her so much. They then decided to "share" her. The three of them moved in together, later on forming a "family partnership". They eventually had four children together (the story behind it is very interesting). Because of their unique three-way partnership family, she has gotten to know other couples where a third person was regularly a part of their intimate relationships.

It is the correspondence to/from these other advocates of three-way intimacy relationships that Joan's true reports are based on. And yes, it can happen... It can be very fun, intimate, and wonderful!

"Thank you for reading my stories/reports. If you are part of a three-way intimate relationship, I would love to hear from you." -Joan-

From the Author

"Thank you for reading my stories/reports. If you are part of a three-way intimate relationship, I would love to hear from you."

Check my page on Amazon and my blog for Updates and interesting info.

Author Central Page - http://amzn.to/14ZEmfs

Author Blog - http://joan-vegas.awesomeauthors.org/

If you enjoyed any of my books then please share the love and click like on my books in Amazon.

If you write me a review and send me an email I will send you a free book, or many.
(Just know that these emails are filtered by my publisher.)

Good news is always welcome.

One Last Thing, For Kindle Readers...

When you turn the page, Kindle will give you the opportunity to rate this book and share your thoughts on Facebook and Twitter. If you enjoyed my writings, would you please take a few seconds to let your friends know about it? Because... when they enjoy they will be grateful to you and so will I.

Thank You!

Joan Vegas
joan_vegas@awesomeauthors.org